OXFORD BOOKWORM
True Stories

Ellis Island

Rosalia's Story

JANET HARDY-GOULD

Stage 2 (700 headwords)

Illustrated by Thomas Girard

Series Editor: Rachel Bladon
Founder Editors: Jennifer Bassett
and Tricia Hedge

OXFORD

UNIVERSITY PRESS

Great Clarendon Street, Oxford, OX2 6DP, United Kingdom

Oxford University Press is a department of the University of Oxford.
It furthers the University's objective of excellence in research, scholarship,
and education by publishing worldwide. Oxford is a registered trade
mark of Oxford University Press in the UK and in certain other countries

ISBN: 978 0 19 463444 1

A complete recording of this Bookworms edition
of *Ellis Island: Rosalia's Story* is available.

Printed in China

Word count (main text): 8,707

For more information on the Oxford Bookworms Library,
visit www.oup.com/elt/gradedreaders

ACKNOWLEDGEMENTS

Cover images by: Getty Images/Shanina; Shutterstock/Boumen Japet/
art of line/Melok/jcwait/ADragan/VladisChern.

Main illustrations by: Thomas Girard/Good Illustration.

Other illustrations by: Martin Sanders/Beehive Illustration (map).

The publisher would like to thank the following for permission to
reproduce photographs: Alamy Stock Photo pp.58 (immigrants showing
passports/Everett Collection Historical), 58 (female immigrants
examination/Everett Collection Inc), 58 (Immigration Station/Hi-Story);
Getty Images pp.56 (Registry Room/Patti McConville), 58 (Ellis Island/
Archive Holdings Inc.), 67 (Charlie Chaplin/Imagno).

The publisher would like to thank Barry Moreno, Historian at the
Ellis Island National Museum of Immigration, New York City, for his help
with this book.

CONTENTS

MAP: JOURNEY FROM PALERMO
AND NAPLES TO NEW YORK   iv

1   Brooklyn, New York, 1925 (Part 1)   1

2   Leaving Sicily   4

3   Life on Board   12

4   New Friends   20

5   The Necklace   28

6   The Atlantic   33

7   Ellis Island   37

8   The Registry Room   45

9   Brooklyn, New York, 1925 (Part 2)   51

GLOSSARY   53

STORY NOTES   55

BEYOND THE STORY   56

PHOTOS OF ELLIS ISLAND   58

ACTIVITIES: Think Ahead   59

ACTIVITIES: Chapter Check   60

ACTIVITIES: Focus on Vocabulary   64

ACTIVITIES: Focus on Language   65

ACTIVITIES: Discussion   66

PROJECT   67

RECOMMENDED READING   68

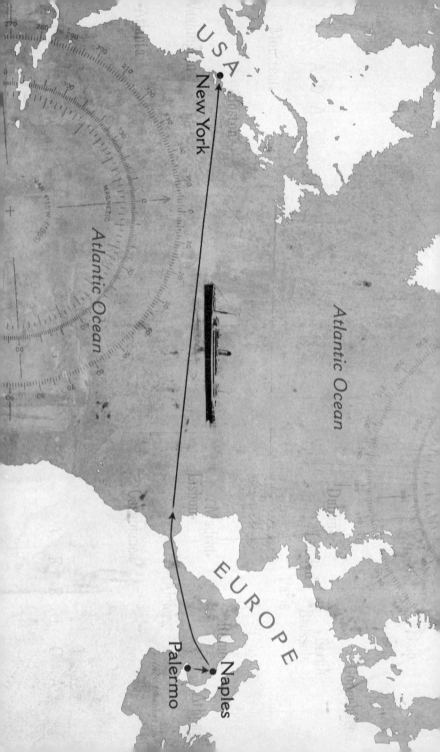

CHAPTER ONE

Brooklyn, New York, 1925 (Part 1)

My friend has just visited us in our new apartment in Brooklyn, and now I need to begin unpacking. There are boxes all around me, which are full of clothes, books, and kitchen things. The children are climbing all over them, and laughing or shouting.

"Be careful, you two!" I say, and then I begin to take the things out of one of the boxes. There are a lot of letters and books inside it. I have not looked at these things for years, so it is a big surprise when I see my old red sketchbook. I remember it immediately, and quickly open it. On the first page, there is a note:

Spadafora, Sicily   *November 1, 1910*

Dear Rosalia,

Here's a sketchbook for your voyage to America. Draw a picture in it every day on the ship, and think of me. I'll never forget you.

Your friend,
Nicoletta

I remember Nicoletta's smiling face, and I think, "Where is she now? Is she still back in Italy?"

But a voice in my ear brings me back to here and now, and my daughter, Giovanna, pulls at the book.

"Mommy, Mommy! What's that in your hand?" she asks.

"It's my old sketchbook," I say. "With my drawings in it."

"Can we look at it?" asks my son, Matteo.

"Yes, of course," I answer. So Giovanna and Matteo come and sit next to me, and we begin looking through it together.

"Who are these people?" asks Giovanna when she sees the first drawing.

"Those two people are my grandparents, and that girl was my best friend, Nicoletta," I answer.

"Oh yes," says Matteo. "You told us about them."

"But where are they in the picture?" asks Giovanna.

"They're on the island of Sicily – you know, I was born there. And they're all saying goodbye to me at the docks when I came here to America by ship fifteen years ago."

"Let's show the book to Daddy when he gets home from the office," says Giovanna.

"Yes," I smile. "I know that he'll be very interested."

They run away to play. I watch them, but I am thinking about something different. I am thinking about my voyage here long ago.

"It's my old sketchbook."

CHAPTER TWO
Leaving Sicily

Everything began with a letter from our father in America. He was already in New York and he wrote to us in Sicily with news.

The letter arrived on October 4, the day before my fourteenth birthday. I remember it well. Mother went and sat at the table in our kitchen with the letter in her hand. My four-year-old brother, Arturo, and I came to sit next to her, while ten-month-old Sebastiano lay in his small bed. Mother opened the letter, but just then, Sebastiano began to cry.

"Can you hold him, Rosalia?" Mother asked. So I took him in my arms, and Mother read the letter to us.

New York   *September 1, 1910*

Dear Piera, Rosalia, Arturo, and Sebastiano,

I'm writing to you with good news! At last, after seven months, I have the money to bring you here to America. So I bought you tickets for the ship The Napolitan Princess. *It leaves Sicily on November 2, and it will arrive in New York about three weeks later. I'll meet you at Ellis Island when you get off the ship.*

Mother read the letter to us.

"Where's Ellis Island?" I asked, and Mother stopped reading and looked up.

"It's a small island near New York," she explained. "People arrive there when they want to live in America, and they have health checks, and answer lots and lots of questions." Then she read some more:

I haven't found us a place to live yet. Right now,
I'm working long hours at the clothes factory. But
in the next few weeks, I'll try to find somewhere.

Mother looked up. "Poor Father has to work in that
dirty factory now," she said.

"Poor Father!" said Arturo, and he took Mother's
hand.

My father had a shoemaking business in Sicily before
he left for New York. He had a beautiful store in our
village, and rich people came from the city of Messina
to buy his shoes. But in 1908, there was a big earthquake.
Lots of people died, and after that, nobody had any
money for shoes, clothes, or even food. So Father went
to America, to look for a new job.

Mother went on reading the letter:

You need to know some important things
about the voyage. When you first go on the ship,
the officials will ask you lots of questions, like,
"Where are you from?" and "Why are you going to
America?" You need to give the right answers. Also,
I only had money for steerage tickets – the cheapest
ones. So you'll be on the lower deck of the ship
with hundreds of other passengers, and you'll sleep
in a room with a lot of other people. But you'll be
all right, I'm sure.

You can only bring two suitcases – nothing more. But remember, winters are very cold here and you'll need warm clothes. Also, be careful with money, rings, or necklaces because people sometimes steal things on board.

I want you to come very soon, so I bought you tickets for November. There can be storms in the Atlantic in the winter months and the voyage is often difficult. But I know that you won't be afraid.

Eat well and stay away from people who are sick while you are on board. I don't want to worry you, but when you arrive at Ellis Island, there are doctors with hooks. They use these hooks to open your eyes and look for infections. Two passengers on my ship had an eye infection called trachoma, so the doctors sent them back to Italy!

"Doctors with hooks!" I said. "That sounds terrible!"

"Shh…" Mother said quietly, and she looked at Arturo. But he was watching a bird outside, so she went on reading.

I'll say goodbye now. But I send you my love, and I'll write again soon.

Your husband and father,
Carlo

Mother put the letter away. "Well," she said, looking at me, "we leave in four weeks, so we need to begin making plans."

A month later, on November 2, we were at the busy docks in Palermo, far from our village. The weather was warm and sunny, but we were wearing heavy winter clothes because our suitcases were full.

"I'm hot in this coat and hat," I said to Mother. "I want to take them off now."

"No," she said. "Keep them on. You can take them off when you get on board."

We were standing with our grandparents. They looked old and worried in the large crowds of people. Grandfather had Sebastiano. Grandmother held Arturo's hand.

"Look at that big ship, Arturo," she said, and she looked up at *The Napolitan Princess* and tried to smile. "It's going to take you to America!"

She took some sweets from her bag and gave them to Arturo. "Here's something for the journey," she said. Then she took out a box and gave it to me. "This is for you, Rosalia."

In the box was a gold necklace. "It belonged to my mother," she explained. "Wear it, and think of us in Sicily."

"Thank you!" I said. "It's beautiful!"

In the box was a gold necklace.

Just then, I heard my name. Someone was calling me. I turned and saw my friend, Nicoletta.

"Nicoletta!" I said happily. "What are you doing here?"

"I came with my father," she laughed. "He was bringing some vegetables to the market here in Palermo."

She saw the box in my hand.

"I have a present for you, too," she said, and she gave me a bag. Inside, there was a sketchbook and a pencil. She knew that I loved drawing.

"It's for the voyage," she said. "You can draw everything on board."

"Thank you, Nicoletta. I'll always—" I began, but suddenly, we heard the ship's horn.

"We have to go now!" said Mother.

She took Sebastiano from Grandfather, and, still holding the bag with the sketchbook and pencil, I took Arturo's hand. My grandparents put their arms around us one last time. Then Mother and I took the two suitcases and hurried to the ship. I could see Grandmother out of the corner of my eye – she was crying.

We walked up the gangplank onto the ship, behind a line of people, and followed them to a desk with an official behind it. "You must give true answers to these questions," he said, and he began to ask Mother many different things.

"Where were you born?" he started. "And where were your children born?" Mother tried to answer carefully, but her voice was shaking. The official listened and wrote her answers on a large piece of paper.

"Are you going to meet family in America?" he asked, and "Have you ever been to prison?"

"All these strange questions!" I thought.

But at last, he said, "That's fine."

We walked up to the top of the ship, and out onto the open deck, and looked down at the crowds below. I could see my grandparents and Nicoletta – they looked

so small. Then I remembered the sketchbook and pencil.
I took them out of the bag and began to draw.

"I want one last picture," I thought. "To remember
my old life here in Sicily."

"*I want one
last picture,*"
I thought.

CHAPTER THREE
Life on Board

We heard the sound of the horn again, and then the ship began to move slowly away from the docks. I finished drawing, and looked up at Mother next to me. Arturo was holding her hand, and Sebastiano was asleep in her arms. There were tears in her eyes.

The crowds of people below waved and cheered. I could see Nicoletta. She was jumping up and down wildly and shouting, "Goodbye!" Grandfather was waving his newspaper. Grandmother was holding his arm and trying not to cry.

At first, we called and waved, too, but after a while, we could not hear the people's voices or see their faces anymore. The streets of Palermo looked smaller and smaller, and soon, we began to see all the high mountains behind the city.

"All steerage passengers down below decks!" a sailor shouted.

"That's us," said Mother. We walked with many other passengers down some stairs, and came to a half-open door. Inside, we saw a bright room with comfortable chairs and a colorful carpet.

"That looks nice!" I said to Mother. "Is it for us?"

"No," she replied quickly. "That's for the first-class passengers."

Arturo and I followed Mother, with Sebastiano in her arms, down some more stairs. They were narrower than the first ones, and it got darker and darker when we went down. At last, we arrived at one of the lower decks. A sailor was standing there.

"Steerage?" he said to Mother.

"Yes," she answered.

"Women and children, this way," he said, and showed us an open door.

"Thank you," Mother smiled. But when she looked through the door, the smile suddenly left her face. There, in front of us, was a large, dark cabin full of old bunk beds. The floor and walls were very dirty. Some other passengers were already sitting on their beds, so we walked around and looked for some empty places.

"Let's go to that corner," said Mother, and she pointed to two empty bunk beds. We walked across the cabin to them, then sat on the bottom beds with our suitcases. The beds felt hard and uncomfortable, and the pillows were old and dirty.

For a while, we sat silently. We looked around at everything, and listened to the noise of all the people in the cabin. The ship was moving up and down a lot more now, and some of the passengers were already feeling ill, I could see: they were lying on their beds, and their faces were white. I did not want to say anything to my mother, but I suddenly felt very worried and afraid.

There was a large, dark cabin full of old bunk beds.

We looked around, and I found a bathroom next to our cabin with places to wash and a few toilets.

"Are these for everybody in our cabin?" I whispered to Mother.

"Yes," she said. "But it's only for three weeks."

Early that evening, we had our first meal. We sat around tables at the far end of our cabin with all the other women and children. The ship's cooks gave us all brown soup. I took a mouthful of it.

"What's in this?" I asked Mother. "I can't eat it."

"We have to finish the food, or we'll be hungry later," she whispered, and she tried to give Sebastiano some soup.

I held my nose and finished the soup. Then I looked at the other passengers. There were lots of little children, but only one girl who was older – and she was sitting at the next table. She had long, dark hair and wore old clothes, and she had two brothers, like me. They called her name – it was Carolina. I looked at her and smiled, but she did not smile back. She just looked down tiredly.

After dinner, most of us went and sat on our beds and read or talked. I looked at the empty beds in our cabin, and said to Mother, "The ship isn't very full, is it? That's good."

"More passengers will get on when we arrive in Naples," she said. "Now, come on. Get ready for bed."

"But where can I change my clothes?" I asked.

"Here," she said.

"What? In front of everybody?"

"I'll hold this blanket around you," she said. "Nobody is looking at you." So I quickly put on my nightclothes, got into the bunk bed above Arturo, and took off my gold necklace and put it under my pillow. Mother got into the bottom of the next bed with baby Sebastiano.

I lay there quietly, but I could not sleep. The ship made strange noises, and I did not like moving up and down all the time. Two babies were crying loudly and an old woman was talking in her sleep.

I thought about Sicily and my favorite places there – Nicoletta's little house with fruit trees in the garden, and the store in our village with bread in the window. I wanted to be back in my comfortable bed at home, with my things all around me. It was very late when I fell asleep.

When I woke up the next morning, I could not remember where I was. Our cabin smelled of last night's dinner, and I looked in surprise at the strange people around me. I put my hand under my pillow and found my necklace there.

"Come on, Rosalia!" said Mother. "Time for breakfast!"

I put my head under my blanket. "I don't want breakfast!" I answered.

"You have to eat something," she said.

I climbed down from the bunk bed, got dressed, and we went and sat at the tables with all the other people from the cabin. Soon, we were eating gray oatmeal. "This doesn't taste like anything," I said unhappily.

But I ate the oatmeal, and after breakfast, I began to feel more excited about our adventure.

"Can I look around the ship now?" I asked Mother.

"Yes," she said. "But take Arturo with you, and be very careful."

In the dark corridor next to our cabin, we saw Carolina and her younger brother. She looked away when I smiled at her, and Arturo and I walked past her. We began to climb the stairs to the higher decks, but a sailor stood in our way.

"I'm sorry," he said, "but you can't go up on the open deck. Only first-class passengers can go there in the mornings. You can go there for an hour in the afternoons."

We went back down the stairs. "Where can I play, then?" Arturo asked me.

"In the cabin, maybe?" I said.

"But there are too many people there!" Arturo said. "And it smells!"

We walked back down the corridor, and Arturo began to cry. There was no one in the corridor outside our cabin, and I saw a door at the far end, and opened it carefully. "Maybe there's another room in here!" I said.

The door did not open into a room, but into a very large closet with a light. There were some boxes in one corner, but you could walk around in it.

"Look, Arturo!" I said. "Maybe you can play in here.

It can be our secret place! We won't tell anyone."

Arturo's face lit up, and he ran into the closet and jumped around.

"Thank you, Rosalia!" he smiled, and I put my arms around him.

Arturo ran into the closet and jumped around.

The next morning, I walked around the cabin and corridor with Arturo, played with him in the secret closet, and made sketches. The other passengers talked and played cards on their beds.

In the afternoon, all the steerage passengers could go up on the open deck for an hour. The sun and wind on our faces were wonderful after our dark, noisy cabin with its bad smell and crowds of passengers. But I felt lonely without any friends. I smiled at Carolina when I saw her, but she did not smile back.

Later that afternoon, the ship stopped at Naples and the sailors said that we could go on the open deck again. I took my sketchbook and drew the docks and the big crowds below.

While I was drawing, the new passengers began walking up the gangplank, and out of the corner of my eye, I saw a girl in a green dress with lots of wild, brown hair and big eyes. She was walking with a boy, and he looked just like her. They were both about fourteen, I thought. They looked up, and when they saw me, they smiled, and I smiled back.

"Oh, good!" I thought. "Some friends."

CHAPTER FOUR
New Friends

D inner that evening was very busy, because of all the new passengers from Naples. The girl in the green dress was at a dinner table near us. She was eating her meal very slowly. When she saw me, she pointed at the food and made a funny face. I laughed.

Later, I saw her on a bunk bed on my side of the cabin, so I went to talk to her.

"Welcome to our cabin!" I said. "What's your name?"

"Angelina Di Pietro," she said. "What about you?"

"I'm Rosalia Lorino," I said. "I'm from Spadafora."

"I'm from near Castellabate," she said.

She spoke a little differently from me, but I could easily understand her. I wanted to talk more, but just then, my mother called me because she was putting my brothers to bed and needed some help.

"See you tomorrow, maybe?" I asked.

"Yes," she said, smiling.

The next morning, Angelina was not on her bed when I got up. I saw Carolina, but as usual, she did not smile at me, so I went to look for Angelina, and found her outside the dirty, smelly toilets.

"How was your first night?" I asked. I held my nose because of the terrible smell.

"I slept very badly," she said. "It's so noisy in the

cabin, isn't it? Can you sleep?"

"It was hard at first," I answered. "But I'm so tired now. I fell asleep right away last night."

Angelina looked around at all the people who were waiting to use the toilets, and asked, "How do you get away from everyone during the day?"

I knew that Arturo would like Angelina, so I decided to tell her about the closet. "I know a secret place," I said. "I'll take you there now if you want."

Angelina's eyes lit up. "A secret place?" she said. "How exciting! Can I ask my twin brother, Vincenzo, too? He's in the men's cabin because we're fourteen. But he doesn't know anybody there."

"Of course," I replied. "I'll bring my little brother, Arturo, too. See you by the cabin door."

I quickly went to find Arturo, then hurried back to the cabin door, and the twins were already waiting there.

"This is Arturo," I said.

"And this is my twin brother, Vincenzo," said Angelina.

"Pleased to meet you," he smiled.

Angelina and Vincenzo followed Arturo and me to the secret closet.

"This is great!" said Vincenzo, when we were inside.

"It's Arturo's secret place, isn't it, Arturo?" I said.

"Well, Arturo, I like your secret place very much!" laughed Vincenzo, and Arturo smiled happily.

Arturo had two little soldiers, and he began playing

with them in the corner. Vincenzo took out some cards, and he, Angelina, and I played a game and talked.

"This is better than our cabin!" laughed Angelina.

"Yes!" I agreed. I dropped a card, and when I moved to get it, the end of my necklace fell out from my dress. "What a beautiful necklace!" Angelina said.

"Thanks. My grandmother gave it to me."

"Is she on the ship?" asked Angelina.

"No, she's in Sicily. She was unhappy when we left. But she knows that we need to start a new life in New York. My poor father lost his business after the earthquake, you see. He was a shoemaker."

"That's hard for your family," said Vincenzo. "Our father was a barber – he cut people's hair in Castellabate. But he didn't get a lot of money for his work, and he thought that he would get more in America."

"Yes, we heard our parents sometimes when they talked about it at night," said Angelina. "They were very worried about money. So, in the end, our father decided to go to New York and then bring us there later."

"That's what our father did, too," I said, and I put down my last card.

"You won!" they laughed, and Vincenzo got ready for another game.

"Look at this," said Angelina. She took something out of her pocket – it was a page from a newspaper with photos of New York on it.

It was a page from a newspaper with photos of New York on it.

"That's the Statue of Liberty," she said, pointing to one picture. "We'll see it when we arrive."

"Really?" I said, and I looked at the picture excitedly. It was a statue of a woman, and she looked tall and strong.

"And that's Manhattan Island – so many big modern apartment buildings!" Angelina said. "Just think: we'll be there soon!"

"Yes! I'm very excited," I said.

"Can you speak any English?" Angelina asked.

"Only a few words."

"Maybe Vincenzo and I can help you," said Angelina. "Our mother's friend taught us some English – she's a teacher. And Vincenzo has an old English book – he studies with it all the time."

"Yes," said Vincenzo. "I'm going to work very hard at my English in New York, too. Our father has a job as a builder there. I want to work with him during the day, but I'm going to study English at night, because then I can get good work in an office."

"I'd like to be a dressmaker," said Angelina, smiling brightly. "I've already begun to learn. What about you?"

"I don't know," I said. "My father says that some of the jobs in New York are terrible. He works long hours in a dirty factory, and he doesn't get very much money – but he thinks that he'll get a better job soon."

The ship suddenly moved very heavily to one side, and

Vincenzo's cards all fell across the floor of the closet.

"I'm not worried about being in New York," said Vincenzo. "But I *am* worried about the voyage. In a few days, we'll begin crossing the Atlantic. There are stories about ships that have gone down in the stormy seas at this time of year."

"Don't say that!" said Angelina.

"Well, *I'm* worried about Ellis Island," I said. "There are doctors there who open your eyes with hooks."

"No!" said Angelina.

"Yes. They're looking for eye infections," I explained. "If you have an infection, they send you home."

"They sent home a fifteen-year-old boy from Naples last year," said Vincenzo. "He went back alone, without his parents."

"What are you talking about?" said a voice suddenly. We turned and remembered Arturo.

"Let's play another game of cards," I said quickly. "You can help me, Arturo."

After that, Angelina, Vincenzo, Arturo, and I began to go everywhere together. In the mornings, Arturo and I often sat in the secret closet with the twins and talked or played cards – and they taught me some English from Vincenzo's book. But the best time of the day was our hour on the open deck every afternoon, out in the sun, the rain, and the wind.

Mother was soon good friends with Angelina and

Vincenzo's mother, and they often sat and talked for hours. All the adults in the cabin spent their time talking, playing cards, or studying English – and in the evenings, they sometimes sang and danced together.

One afternoon, when Vincenzo came up for our hour on the open deck, he had something under his arm.

"What's that?" I asked.

"It's a soccer ball," he said, and he gave it to me. "One of the sailors gave me an old blanket, and I made a soccer ball from it!" I kicked the soccer ball along the deck to Angelina. To my surprise, it moved very quickly. Arturo and I kicked it around with the twins for a while, and some of the other children came and watched.

"Do you want to play?" Vincenzo asked, and soon, there was a big group of us. Some of the sailors came and played, too – but Carolina just stood and watched.

It was so good to run around. For a while, we forgot that we were on a ship. We forgot that we were on our way to a new life on the other side of the world, and just enjoyed ourselves.

After a while, I stopped playing and made a quick sketch of the game. Vincenzo was in the middle. I wanted to remember his smiling face.

"This is the strangest game of soccer ever – soccer on a ship, with all the sailors!" he shouted to me, his wild, brown hair in his eyes. "I'll always remember this!"

I wanted to remember Vincenzo's smiling face.

"Me too!" I said. I took the bottom of my long dress in my hand and went to kick the ball. Vincenzo ran after it, and I watched him. "Yes, I'll always remember it, too," I thought to myself.

CHAPTER FIVE
The Necklace

When I woke up the next morning and put my hand under my pillow, my gold necklace was not there.

"It dropped on the floor," I thought, but I could not find it. I did not want to tell Mother, because I knew that she would be worried. So I ran to Angelina and she looked for it with me.

"Maybe somebody took it," she whispered.

"Yes," I said, and I thought about Father's letter – maybe he was right about thieves.

Angelina and I went and found Vincenzo, and we explained about the necklace.

"I'm going to find it, Rosalia," he said. "I know that it's important to you."

We looked everywhere, but we could not see it, and I began to feel even more worried.

At lunch, I sat with Angelina, but I did not want to talk. I pushed my food around on my plate: the smell and the noise of the cabin were worse than ever. When I thought about my grandmother, I wanted to cry. "Why wasn't I more careful with the necklace?" I asked myself.

I looked across and saw Carolina. She was finishing her lunch already. "How can she eat it so quickly?" I thought. But then I saw something bright around her neck – it was my necklace.

When I told Angelina, in a whisper, she said, "We need to talk to Carolina. But let's wait until after lunch. And let's ask Vincenzo to come with us."

A little later, Vincenzo, Angelina, and I found Carolina in the corridor near our secret closet. She was still wearing the necklace.

"Carolina, we want to talk to you," I called, and she turned round.

"That's my necklace," I said. "You stole it from me, didn't you?"

"That's my necklace," I said.

"That isn't true!" she replied, and her face went red.

"Yes, it is," I said. "I always keep the necklace under my pillow at night. You took it from there."

"Are you calling me a thief?" shouted Carolina angrily. Then she tried to push me hard. Vincenzo moved in front of me, but Carolina pushed him, and he fell onto the closet door, hitting his face.

We all went to help him, but he stood up with his hand over his eye, and walked away quickly. Angelina ran after him, and Carolina and I were suddenly alone together.

She looked at me, afraid. "I didn't steal the necklace," she said. "I found it on the deck yesterday afternoon. I wanted to give it back, but I didn't know that it was your necklace. I asked lots of the women in the cabin, but no one knew anything about it.

"Here, take it," she said, and she took off the necklace and put it in my hand angrily. "I'm not a thief, you know!"

I understood my mistake, and I felt terrible. I turned and ran to my cabin. Then I got into bed, put the blanket over my head, and began to cry.

"Why did I say those terrible things to Carolina?" I thought. "Why didn't I think carefully first?"

That evening at dinner, I felt very unhappy. I could not find Angelina, and I thought that maybe she and Vincenzo were angry with me, too.

But after dinner, Angelina came to talk to me. She and Vincenzo were not angry, she said. Poor Vincenzo's left eye was hurt, so they had to go with their mother to see the ship's doctor. That was why they were not at dinner. So they were still my friends – and at last, I felt a little better. "I'll go and see Vincenzo!" I said. "But first, I must find Carolina, and say sorry to her."

Carolina was sitting on her bed. "I'm so sorry," I said. "I was wrong about you. You aren't a thief."

"I wanted to give the necklace back," she said. "But I enjoyed wearing it. I've never had anything beautiful like that before."

"Well, thank you for finding it," I said, and to my surprise, she gave me a little smile.

"You don't smile a lot, do you?" I said.

"I don't like meeting new people," she replied. "It's difficult for me."

"I understand," I said, then I stopped and thought. "Would you like to come up on the open deck with us tomorrow?" I asked.

"Yes, I'd like that very much," she smiled.

I knew that I needed to go and find Vincenzo now, so I said goodbye to Carolina and went to look for him. He was in our secret closet, sitting on the floor with Angelina.

His left eye was shut, and dark purple.

"Oh no!" I said. "It will get better soon, won't it?"

Vincenzo's left eye was shut, and dark purple.

"Yes, of course," said Vincenzo. "One of the sailors put some cold meat on it. That's good for a bad eye, he said."

But Angelina looked worried. "Our mother is very afraid," she whispered to me later, when we walked back to the cabin.

"I'm... I'm very sorry," I said.

"Oh, it isn't your fault," said Angelina. But in my head, a voice was saying, "Yes, it is."

CHAPTER SIX
The Atlantic

The next morning, we were just leaving the tables after breakfast when we heard screaming from the other side of the cabin. Mother told me to wait with Arturo and Sebastiano. Then she and Angelina's mother went to see what was happening.

Angelina came and sat on my bed with me and my brothers. "Why was that woman screaming?" she asked.

"I don't know," I said.

A few minutes later, some sailors came into the cabin. There was a lot of talking, and then they left. They were carrying something heavy in a blanket.

"What is it?" I whispered to Angelina.

When my mother came back to our bed, she did not want to talk about the thing in the blanket. "Not in front of Arturo," she whispered to me. But when I walked around the cabin a little later, everyone was talking about it, and I soon knew what was in the blanket. It was the body of a woman who was dead.

"My mother knew the woman," Angelina told me. "She was on the ship with her sister, and my mother met them when we were waiting at the docks in Naples. My mother said that the woman got sick on the ship, and every day, she was worse and worse. When her sister went to see her after breakfast this morning, she was dead. It was the sister who was screaming."

"That's terrible," I said. It was the first death in our cabin, and we talked about it all day. Angelina and I did not want anyone from our families to get sick and die.

But soon, we were worrying about other things, too. "The ship is going to start the voyage across the Atlantic later," one of the other passengers told my mother at breakfast the next day. "And the sailors say that the ocean is very bad right now."

It was true: by the evening, the ship was beginning to crash from side to side, shaking. I saw one of the sailors from the soccer game in the corridor, and he said that we were sailing into a big storm.

"You and your family must go to your beds and stay there," he told me.

That night, the ship moved heavily from side to side for hour after hour. It made the most terrible noises, and in our cabin, tables and chairs crashed across the floor. I felt very afraid. "Is the ship going to go down, and are we all going to die in the Atlantic?" I asked myself.

No one slept that night. Many of the women and children were crying, and a lot of people were very sick. The smell in the cabin was worse than ever.

When morning came at last, we all hoped for a change in the weather, but the storm still pushed the ship around wildly. We stayed on our beds, afraid and sick. Once or twice, when the ocean was quieter for an hour or two, I went to talk to Angelina. She was worried about Vincenzo, in the men's cabin without her and her mother.

Carolina came to see me, too, and she said that her older brother Roberto was very sick. "My mother is so worried about him."

"He'll be OK when the ship comes out of the storm, I'm sure," I said to her.

But Carolina looked very afraid. "I hope so," she said.

For three days, the storm did not stop, but on the fourth morning, the wind and rain were suddenly quieter. Mother, Arturo, and I began to walk around again. We were all happy to be alive.

When I saw Vincenzo, we talked about the terrible storm. His eye was still big and purple, and now the corner of it was a yellow color, too.

"Mother thinks that he has an eye infection," Angelina whispered to me when we were in the cabin later. "And we arrive in New York in four days!"

In the cabin, everyone began to talk about New York, and we were all very excited. Mother got our bags ready, cut our hair, and washed our clothes. "We must look our best for the doctors at Ellis Island," she explained.

"And for Father! I can't wait to see him!" I said.

I wanted to ask her, "Do you think that Father has found an apartment for us?" But I knew that it was best not to say anything. I sometimes heard her when she talked about it in a worried voice to Angelina and Vincenzo's mother.

For these last days of the voyage, Vincenzo, Angelina, Arturo, and I went to the secret closet every morning. Carolina was friends with Vincenzo and Angelina now, too, so she also came, and she sometimes brought her younger brother, Alessandro. Her other brother, Roberto, was still sick, and she and her mother were very worried about him.

"He never gets out of bed," she told us. "My mother was crying last night, because she thinks that the doctors at Ellis Island will send him back to Italy."

We told her not to worry. But poor Carolina often had to go back to the cabin before us, to be with Roberto and her mother, and sometimes she had to stay with them all day.

Vincenzo brought his English book to the secret closet, and he taught me new words every day.

"You're getting good at English, Rosalia," said Angelina. "And Vincenzo, your eye is beginning to look better!"

But when I looked at Vincenzo, I was not sure.

CHAPTER SEVEN
Ellis Island

The last day of our voyage came at last. The passengers packed their suitcases and talked about Ellis Island.

Angelina, Carolina, and I went out to our secret closet for the last time, and we met one of the sailors in the corridor.

"We can see land from the top deck!" he said excitedly.

"Can you see the Statue of Liberty?" Angelina asked.

"Not yet," he said. "The Statue of Liberty is in Upper New York Bay, but we'll come into Lower New York Bay first, and stop there for an hour or two."

"Why?" I asked.

"Officials come on the ship in Lower New York Bay and speak to the first-class passengers," he replied. "They don't have to go through Ellis Island like you."

"Oh, I want to be a first-class passenger!" said Angelina. "They have those nice cabins at the top of the ship for the voyage – and they don't have to go through Ellis Island!"

The sailor was right: the ship stopped a little later. After it began moving again, we went back to the cabin to help our mothers with the suitcases. But the cabin was nearly empty when we got there.

"There you are!" my mother said. "The sailors have said that we can go up onto the open deck. We're arriving in New York!"

We all hurried up to the open deck. There were lots of people at one side of the ship, and we went and stood with them. They were looking up at something, and over their heads, I could just see it: it was the Statue of Liberty. It was so big – and just like in Angelina's picture, the statue held her arm high in the sky, and looked tall and strong.

Many people had tears in their eyes. We were tired, excited, and worried: what kind of life was waiting for us here in New York? Then one of the passengers near us shouted, "She's welcoming us to our new home!"

"A new life in the free world!" shouted another – and suddenly everyone was cheering, crying, and laughing. I quickly took out my sketchbook, and began to draw.

The sailors sent us back down into the cabin after a while, but soon we heard a loud noise and the ship shook. Everyone cheered: we knew that we were coming into the docks.

I felt so happy when I left the dark cabin for the last time and climbed the stairs. At the top, a sailor was standing, smiling. He took our suitcases, then carried them to the gangplank. "Thank you," Mother said. We all looked down: we could see land at last!

"She's welcoming us to our new home!"

"Go across the gangplank and wait down below," the sailor said kindly. "Soon, a boat will take you across to Ellis Island over there. Goodbye and good luck!"

We walked off the gangplank, and for the first time in three weeks, we were on dry land! It was so strange. My head was telling me that I was still on the water, and moving from side to side.

"Go across the gangplank and wait down below."

Poor Vincenzo could not stop touching his eye. "Don't do that, Vincenzo!" said his mother, and she turned to my mother and whispered, "I'm so worried about him."

An official pointed to a small boat and told some of us to go up onto the top deck. Our suitcases went underneath on the lower deck. We could see Carolina and her family on a boat next to us.

The boat began to move slowly across the water to Ellis Island, and we could see the tall apartment buildings on Manhattan Island in front of us.

We stopped at Ellis Island by a big building with large windows. Outside, an American flag was moving in the wind, and some people were waiting.

"They're called the Watchmen," said Vincenzo. "One of the sailors told me about them. They'll take us for our health checks and questions."

We each had a label on our coat or hat – a small piece of paper with our name, the ship's name, and a number. The Watchmen looked at our labels and then put us in groups.

Then each group followed the Watchmen into the building with large windows, and we came to the bottom of some stairs and made a line.

"The sailor told me about this, too," Vincenzo said in a whisper. "When you walk up the stairs, the doctors watch you. They're looking for people who can't walk well."

"When you walk up the stairs, the doctors watch you."

"Walk quickly," said Mother to Arturo and me. "And hold your heads up high." Then she began the long climb up the stairs with Sebastiano in her arms, while Vincenzo waited for Angelina and his mother, who were behind us in the line.

Arturo and I followed our mother, and I felt very afraid. "Are the doctors going to stop us?" I thought. But when we got to the top, and walked in front of them, they did not say a word.

In the line of people in front of us, one of the doctors was talking to Carolina's family. He was standing next to Carolina's older brother, Roberto, and he was looking carefully at Roberto's head, neck, and hands. While we watched, the doctor then wrote something on Roberto's back and sent him to one side. Carolina's mother began crying loudly, and her father shouted angrily at the doctor in Italian.

"What's going to happen to Roberto?" I whispered to Mother. "Will he have to go back to Italy?"

"I don't know," she answered. But she put her arm around Arturo and me, and held Sebastiano nearer. One of the doctors looked at me next, but he quickly waved me past. Then he looked at Mother, Sebastiano, and Arturo, and they were fine, too.

We were through the first health check, and now we followed the other people to some big doors.

"This is the Registry Room," said Mother. "It's the most important place on Ellis Island. Your father told me about it."

We went through the doors, and I looked up in surprise. We were in a very, very big room, and it was full of people who were all talking at once in many different languages.

We got into a line of passengers, and I could see more doctors in front of them.

"Oh no!" I said. "It's the doctors with hooks!"

"Don't worry," said Mother. "Just stand very still while they look at your eyes."

For a very long time, we watched and waited while the

doctors looked at other passengers. I began to feel hot and uncomfortable. Behind me, I could see Vincenzo, Angelina, and their mother. They had worried looks on their faces, and I felt afraid for them, too.

Then, I saw Carolina, her mother, and her brother Alessandro far behind in the crowd. But I could not see her father, or her older brother Roberto. Carolina's mother was still crying, and Carolina and Alessandro looked afraid.

"Poor Carolina!" I thought. I wanted to talk to her, but she was too far away.

We were at the front of the line now, and a doctor pointed at me. I went and stood in front of him, and before I could say anything, he quickly opened my right eye and then my left with the hook.

After that, he looked at Mother and Sebastiano, and Arturo. "You're all fine," he said.

"It was all so quick!" I whispered to Mother.

But when I turned back, Vincenzo was not far behind us, and three doctors were looking worriedly at his left eye. They whispered together, and then one of the doctors held Vincenzo by the arm and took him away.

"Oh no!" I said. "What's going to happen to Vincenzo, Mother?" She turned and looked. "I don't know," she answered quietly, but there were tears in her eyes.

I touched my necklace. "They're going to send Vincenzo home," I thought, "and it's all my fault."

CHAPTER EIGHT
The Registry Room

We had to go to the far end of the Registry Room next. Here, officials sat behind high desks while passengers stood in front of them. Many more passengers sat in the middle of the room. They watched and waited, and when someone called them, they went to see an official.

"How long will we wait?" I asked Mother.

"Three or four hours, maybe," she said. "Father said that it's often very slow."

Sebastiano was crying, and I could not stop thinking about Vincenzo. "Is he all right?" I asked myself again and again.

Every few minutes, I looked around, but I could not see him anywhere. The Registry Room was very noisy, and we were tired and hungry. We sat for a long time and watched while the other passengers went one by one, or with their families, to the end of the room. They stood and answered questions for a few minutes, and then they walked across the Registry Room to some stairs.

"Did they answer all the questions right?" I thought, when the passengers went down the stairs. "And when will they call our name?"

But at last, after three hours, an official shouted, "Family Lorino from Sicily!"

Mother stood up quickly with Sebastiano in her arms, and Arturo and I followed her to the official at his high desk. Another man was standing by the desk. The official looked at some papers in front of him. Then he began to ask us questions. He spoke in English, but the man by the desk listened to the questions and then said them for us in Italian.

The official began to ask us questions.

"Where were you born?" the official asked Mother, his face cold and unsmiling. It was the same questions again – the questions from the beginning of our voyage, when we first got on the ship in Sicily.

"Spadafora, Sicily," Mother answered.

"And you?" he asked in English, pointing at me.

"Me? I... I was born in Spadafora, too," I said in Italian, and the man by the desk then said my words in English.

"No," whispered Mother. "You were born in the next village – that's Rometta."

"Sorry, Rometta," I said loudly.

"Are you sure?" the official asked, and he looked at me for a few seconds.

"Yes," I answered. There was question after question, but at last, the official looked down at us and said, "Go now."

We turned and walked away from the official's desk. "Is that it?" I said to Mother. "Can we live in New York?"

"Yes!" said Mother. "We did it!" She put her arm around me and Arturo, and we laughed happily.

We went across to the stairs, and walked down on the left side, which was the side for anyone who was staying in New York.

Before we left the Registry Room, I looked for Vincenzo and Angelina one last time. "Maybe I will never see them again," I thought.

But I did see someone: Carolina was walking out of the Registry Room, too, with her mother and her brother Alessandro. Her mother was talking to another woman and crying, and Carolina was crying, too. But when she saw me, she hurried across.

"Roberto has to go back to Italy," she said. "Father is going to take him. So Mother, Alessandro, and I will be all alone in New York!"

"Oh, I'm so sorry, Carolina," I said, and held her hand. "We'll meet again, I hope."

"Yes, I'd like that," she answered, and she tried to smile. "You were a good friend to me on the ship. Thank you."

Her mother and brother were looking around for her, so she said goodbye, and then hurried back to them. I felt very sorry for her.

We walked down the stairs, and came to a post office, a ticket office, and a place that was selling American dollars. I began to feel excited. After so many months, I could not wait to see Father. We followed all the other people, and came to a place with another large crowd.

"How are we going to find Father, with all these people here?" I thought. But then we heard a loud shout.

"Piera! Rosalia! Arturo! Sebastiano!" It was my father, and he was running across the room.

When he stood in front of us, he could not speak at

first. He put his arms around us all and pulled us to him. "We're together again!" he said.

I was so excited to see him after all this time, but it was strange, too. He looked older, and tired, and his eyes were full of tears. He took Sebastiano from Mother.

"Look at you, baby Sebastiano! You're a big boy now!" he said, and he began to cry.

"But he isn't as big as me!" said Arturo.

"We're together again!" Father said.

"That's true," replied Father, laughing through his tears.

"Now," he said at last, "I have some good news. I found a very small apartment. It isn't wonderful, but it's a start."

"That's good!" said Mother.

"I have a different job, too," said Father. "I'm helping a shoemaker at the back of a store on Third Avenue. The money isn't good, but I like the work. And maybe one day, I'll have a store again myself.

"I want to hear about the voyage," he went on. "And all your news. But let's go somewhere quieter."

So, we were leaving Ellis Island, and I knew that I would never see Angelina and Vincenzo again. Maybe Vincenzo was getting on the boat back to Italy now – and it was all my fault. I began to cry.

"What's the matter, Rosalia?" asked my father kindly.

I tried to tell him about my friends, the twins, but I could not stop crying.

"Speak more slowly, Rosalia. I don't understand."

My mother began to explain, but then she suddenly stopped and said, "Look, Rosalia!"

We all turned around in surprise. There was Vincenzo. He was walking up to us with Angelina and their mother. I closed my eyes, then opened them, and he was still there.

I smiled, then tried to speak, but no words came out.

CHAPTER NINE

Brooklyn, New York, 1925 (Part 2)

" That feels like a very long time ago," I think, when I sit and look again at the last pictures of my voyage to New York in my sketchbook.

I laugh when I see my picture of the soccer game on the open deck, and I smile when I come to the last drawing – the Statue of Liberty.

"That isn't my best picture!" I think. "I couldn't draw very well because I was so cold, worried, and excited – all at the same time!"

I hear the sound of a key in the front door of our apartment.

"Daddy is home!" says Matteo excitedly.

The children run to the front door. "Hello, Daddy!" they call.

"Hello," he says. "Have you had a good day? Did Angelina and Carolina come and visit our new apartment?"

"Carolina came this morning," I say. "But Angelina was busy. She's going to come tomorrow."

"Mommy found her old sketchbook," says Matteo, and he points at the book in my hand.

"Can I have a look at it?" he asks.

"Of course," I smile. "Come and sit down, Vincenzo. I think that you're going to enjoy looking at this!"

"Hello, Daddy!"

apartment *(n)* a group of rooms to live in, on one floor of a larger building

blanket *(n)* a warm cover for a bed

bunk bed *(n)* a bed that is usually above another bed

cabin *(n)* a room for sleeping on a ship

cards *(n)* a group of 52 small pieces of heavy paper, with numbers on; you use them to play games

cheer *(v)* to give a loud shout because you are happy or think that something is good

city *(n)* a big and important town

corridor *(n)* a long, narrow walkway that takes you from one room to another

deck *(n)* one of the floors of a ship or airplane

dock *(n)* At a dock, a ship stops and passengers get on or off.

draw *(v)* to make a picture with a pen or a pencil; **drawing** *(n)*

earthquake *(n)* a sudden strong shaking of the ground

fault *(n)* a mistake; something bad that happens because of you

first-class *(adj)* having a ticket that means you can travel in the best or most expensive part of a ship, train, or airplane

flag *(n)* a piece of cloth or paper on a stick with special colors or pictures for a country

game *(n)* something you play, like soccer or cards

gangplank *(n)* a kind of bridge that goes from the side of a boat to the ground

health check *(n)* when a doctor or nurse looks at someone's body because they want to know that the person is not ill

hook *(n)* a thin stick with a rounded end like a "C"

horn *(n)* a thing, for example on a ship or a car, that makes a loud sound when you push it

infection *(n)* when you have an illness in one part of your body

kick *(v)* to hit somebody or something with your foot

land *(n)*   the part of the Earth that is not water; a piece of ground

line *(n)*   a group of people who are standing one behind the other, waiting to do something

lower *(adj)*   below one or more things

necklace *(n)*   a long, thin thing (often expensive) that you wear round your neck because it looks nice

oatmeal *(n)*   a soft, hot food for breakfast

official *(n)*   a person who does important work, often for an important group of people or a country

on board *(adv)*   on or onto a ship, train, bus, or airplane

parent *(n)*   a mother or father

pillow *(n)*   a soft thing that you put your head on when you are in bed

point *(v)*   to hold up your finger or a stick to show something

sketch *(n)*   a picture that you make quickly with a pencil

soup *(n)*   food that is like a thick drink; to make it, you cook things like vegetables or meat in water

statue *(n)*   a stone or metal model of a person or animal

tear *(n)*   a drop of water that comes from your eye when you cry

twin *(n)*   a brother and sister or two brothers/sisters who were born at the same time

voyage *(n)*   a long journey by boat or ship

wave *(v)*   to move your hand from side to side or up and down to say hello or goodbye to someone

welcome *(v)*   to show someone that you are happy to see them when they arrive at a place

whisper *(v & n)*   to say something very quietly

Atlantic a large ocean between America and Europe

Brooklyn a place in New York City, south of Manhattan Island

Castellabate a town in southwest Italy

Ellis Island a small island near New York City; many immigrants came here when they first arrived in America

Lower New York Bay a place in the sea below Upper New York Bay and east of Brooklyn

Manhattan Island the most important and busiest place in New York City

Messina a city on the island of Sicily

Naples a large city in the south of Italy

Palermo the most important city in Sicily

Registry Room a large room on Ellis Island; immigrants (people who came to live in America from other countries) had to answer questions here when they first arrived

Sicily a big island in the Mediterranean, near Italy

Spadafora a village near Messina in Sicily

Statue of Liberty a famous 93-meter statue of a woman that stands on an island very near New York City

Third Avenue a long street on Manhattan Island, New York

Upper New York Bay a place in the sea around Ellis Island, near New York City

Watchmen people who worked on Ellis Island and helped the officials there

Ellis Island

Ellis Island is a small island near New York City in the USA. It is famous because, from 1892 to 1954, more than 12 million immigrants stopped there during their journey to America. Many of the people who stopped at Ellis Island came from Europe. Often, they were leaving dangerous or very poor places and they wanted to start a new, better life in America. Immigrants to America also traveled by ship from Europe to different cities – like Boston, Baltimore, Miami, and New Orleans – but most of them went to Ellis Island and New York City.

When the ships arrived in New York, passengers who had first-class tickets could travel immediately into the city. Passengers with cheaper, steerage tickets got off at Ellis Island. Officials on the island then gave the passengers health checks and questioned them. Most of the immigrants who arrived on Ellis Island stayed for three to five hours and could then go into America. But others spent many days or weeks on the island, and around 2%

of the people who arrived at Ellis Island could not go into America, and had to go home.

After they traveled through Ellis Island, the new immigrants often stayed to live and work in New York, or took trains from the stations in Hoboken or Jersey City to cities and towns across America.

Today, there is a museum on Ellis Island and around two million visitors go there every year. Visitors can look over the water from the island and see many of New York's famous places, like the Statue of Liberty and the tall buildings on Manhattan Island. They can also learn the stories of some of the people who came to America. They hear about people like Annie Moore, the first immigrant who went through Ellis Island. She left Ireland with her two brothers on a ship called *Nevada* and met her parents in New York on January 1, 1892. She was seventeen years old when she arrived in America.

READ & RESEARCH Read 'Beyond the Story' and research the answers to these questions.

1 When was the busiest year for Ellis Island?

2 Who was the last immigrant to go through Ellis Island?

3 Sigmund Freud, Harry Houdini, and Albert Einstein all came to America through Ellis Island. What countries did they come from and why are they famous?

immigrant *(n)* a person who comes to live in a country from another country

museum *(n)* In a museum, you can look at old and interesting things.

PHOTOS OF ELLIS ISLAND

Passengers see the Statue of Liberty

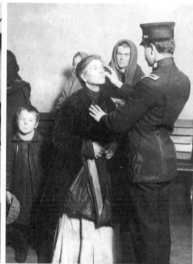

A doctor checks people's eyes

An official asks questions

The Registry Room

Think Ahead

1 Read the back cover and the contents page. How much do you know about the story? Check (✓) the true sentences.

1 Rosalia moves to America. ☐

2 Rosalia was born in 1910. ☐

3 Rosalia travels across the Atlantic on a ship. ☐

4 Rosalia makes friends on the ship. ☐

2 Imagine it is the year 1910 and you are moving to the USA from another country. Answer the questions.

1 You will never go back to your old country. Who are the people that you will never see again?

2 You can only take two suitcases. What will you pack to remember your old life?

3 You do not speak English and have never seen a city before. How will you feel when you arrive in New York City?

3 **RESEARCH** Find answers to these questions about Ellis Island.

1 Where is Ellis Island?

2 Why is Ellis Island famous?

3 What can you see if you visit Ellis Island today?

Chapter Check

CHAPTER 1 Are the sentences true or false?

1 Rosalia is looking in the boxes because she has moved to a new apartment.

2 Rosalia often looks at her old red sketchbook.

3 The sketchbook was from Rosalia's friend, Nicoletta.

4 Rosalia knows that Nicoletta is in Italy.

5 Rosalia looks through the sketchbook with her children.

6 Fifteen years ago, Rosalia left Italy and traveled to America by ship.

CHAPTER 2 Complete the sentences with the correct words.

1908   in winter   November 2   October 5   three weeks

1 _____ is Rosalia's birthday.

2 The ship from Sicily to New York took about _____.

3 People in Sicily were poorer after the earthquake of _____.

4 Traveling across the Atlantic in a ship was more dangerous _____.

5 On _____, Rosalia got two presents: one from her grandmother and one from her friend.

CHAPTER 3 Put sentences a–f in the correct order.

a More passengers got onto the ship.

b The family had breakfast.

c Rosalia went to the cabin for the first time.

d Rosalia and Arturo found a closet.

e The ship left Palermo.

f Rosalia changed her clothes behind a blanket.

CHAPTER 4 Check (✓) the four correct sentences.

1 Rosalia was soon friends with Carolina. ☐

2 Rosalia showed Vincenzo and Angelina the closet. ☐

3 Angelina's and Rosalia's fathers thought that they could make more money in America than in Italy. ☐

4 Rosalia was excited about seeing America. ☐

5 Rosalia's favorite time of day was when she played cards. ☐

6 Rosalia drew a group of people playing soccer. ☐

CHAPTER 5 Match the sentence halves.

1 In the morning, Rosalia woke up...

2 Carolina was wearing the necklace, ...

3 Carolina pushed Vincenzo...

4 Rosalia took the necklace...

5 After dinner, Angelina talked to Rosalia, ...

6 Rosalia went to the closet...

a and he hit his face on a door.

b and saw Vincenzo's badly hurt eye.

c and couldn't find her necklace.

d and Rosalia thought that she was a thief.

e and Rosalia decided to say sorry to Carolina.

f and went to her bed to cry.

CHAPTER 6 Put sentences a–f in the correct order.

a Rosalia's family got ready to arrive in New York.

b Some sailors carried away a woman's body.

c After breakfast, Rosalia heard someone screaming.

d Rosalia saw Vincenzo's eye, and the corner of it
   was yellow.

e The friends went to the secret closet and talked about
   Carolina's brother.

f During the terrible storm, Rosalia stayed in bed.

CHAPTER 7 Choose the correct words.

1 The *first-class / steerage* passengers got off before Ellis Island.

2 The small boat took Rosalia and her family to *Ellis Island / Manhattan Island*.

3 The people who took everyone for their health checks on Ellis Island were called *Watchmen / officials*.

4 Each passenger from the ship wore a *label / hat*.

5 Doctors with hooks looked at people's *eyes / hands*.

CHAPTER 8 Are the sentences true or false?

1 Rosalia could see Vincenzo from the far end of the Registry Room.

2 Rosalia was born in Spadafora.

3 Carolina cried because some of her family could not go to New York.

4 Rosalia's father had a new apartment and a new job.

5 Vincenzo had to go back to Italy.

CHAPTER 9 Complete the text with the names.

Angelina   Carolina   Matteo   Rosalia   Vincenzo

Rosalia and ¹_____ married and now live with their children, Giovanna and ²_____. When ³_____ looks at her sketchbook, she thinks that the journey to New York feels like a very long time ago. She often sees her friends from the ship: ⁴_____ visited the new apartment today and ⁵_____ will visit tomorrow.

Focus on Vocabulary

1 Complete the sentences with the words.

bunk bed   cabin   deck   flag   gangplank   pillow

1 The _____ on the bed was old and dirty, so
  Rosalia didn't want it to touch her head.

2 Rosalia only saw the sun when she went to the open
  _____.

3 The new passengers walked onto the ship along the
  _____.

4 Their _____ on the ship was dark and full
  of people.

5 Rosalia got into the _____ above Arturo and
  tried to go to sleep.

6 At Ellis Island, they saw an American _____
  moving in the wind.

2 Replace the <u>underlined</u> words with the words below.

cheered   drew   kicked   waved   whispered

1 "Maybe someone took your necklace!" she <u>said quietly</u>.

2 When they arrived in New York, they <u>shouted happily</u>.

3 I took out my pencil and <u>made a picture of</u> Ellis Island.

4 "Goodbye!" I said, and <u>moved my hand from side to side</u>.

5 The ball came to him and he <u>hit</u> it <u>with his foot</u>.

Focus on Language

1 Complete the sentences with *looked, sounded,* or *felt*.

My father told me about the doctors' hooks. They
___*sounded*___ terrible.

1 There were lots of people in the cabin, but I
_____ lonely without any friends.

2 "I'm OK," my mother said. But I saw her face, and she
_____ very tired.

3 I lay on the bed. It _____ hard and
uncomfortable.

4 The Statue of Liberty _____ tall and strong.

5 I could hear people shouting on the open deck – they
_____ happy.

**2 DECODE Read this text from the story and <u>underline</u> the
words *her, his,* and *him*.**

Mother stood up quickly with Sebastiano in her arms, and
Arturo and I followed her to the official at his high desk.
Another man was standing by the desk. The official looked
at some papers in front of him.

**3 Match the <u>underlined</u> words from exercise 2 to the
meanings below.**

1 my mother   3 the official

2 my mother's   4 the official's

Discussion

1 **THINK CRITICALLY** Read the discussion. Who do you agree with most, Speaker A or Speaker B?

   A: I think that the most difficult time in Rosalia's journey was when she left Sicily.

   B: Why's that?

   A: She left her grandparents and knew that she wouldn't see them again.

   B: Oh, I don't agree. I think that the most difficult time was when she went through Ellis Island.

   A: Why do you think that?

   B: Because her family had to have lots of health checks, and she was worried about her friend Vincenzo.

2 Look at the conversation in exercise 1 again. Which two questions are used to get more information?

3 Think about Rosalia's journey. Put these things in order, from hardest to easiest.

   saying goodbye to Sicily   seeing the cabin for the first time
   losing her necklace   the storm in the Atlantic
   going through Ellis Island   worrying about Vincenzo

4 **COMMUNICATE** Discuss the most difficult time in Rosalia's journey with a partner. Use the questions in exercise 2 to ask for more information.

1 Read this short profile of Charlie Chaplin.

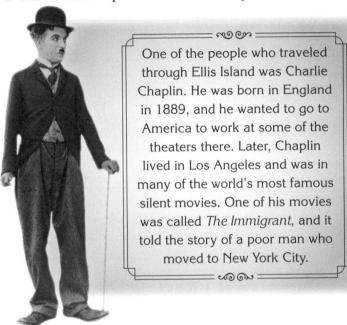

> One of the people who traveled through Ellis Island was Charlie Chaplin. He was born in England in 1889, and he wanted to go to America to work at some of the theaters there. Later, Chaplin lived in Los Angeles and was in many of the world's most famous silent movies. One of his movies was called *The Immigrant*, and it told the story of a poor man who moved to New York City.

2 Answer the questions about Charlie Chaplin.

1 Where was this person born?

2 Why did this person go to America?

3 Where in America did this person live?

4 Why was this person famous?

3 **RESEARCH** Now answer the questions in exercise 2 about another famous person who traveled through Ellis Island.

4 **CREATE** Use your answers from exercise 3 to write a short profile like the one about Charlie Chaplin.

If you liked this Bookworm, why not try...

Amelia Earhart

STAGE 2
Janet Hardy-Gould

"I want to learn to fly," Amelia Earhart tells her family one evening. But it is 1920. Flying is expensive and dangerous, and most people think it is for men, not women.
But nothing can stop Amelia, and she works hard to be a pilot. Soon, she is breaking records for flying further and higher than anyone before. She shows the world that anything is possible – for women and not just men.

Life is always exciting for Amelia. At 41, she is nearly ready to slow down, but she wants to make one last important flight...

New Yorkers – Short Stories

STAGE 2
O. Henry
Retold by Diane Mowat

A housewife, a tramp, a lawyer, a waitress, an actress – ordinary people living ordinary lives in New York at the beginning of the twentieth century. The city has changed greatly since that time, but its people are much the same. Some are rich, some are poor; some are happy, some are sad; some have found love, some are looking for love.

O. Henry's famous short stories give a vivid picture of the everyday lives of these New Yorkers.